W9-CUI-102

Published by KnowWonder Publishing LLC
Kirkland, Washington USA 98034
info@thelandofsmaerd.com

KnowWonder and colophon are trademarks of KnowWonder Publishing LLC
www.KnowWonderEntertainment.com

Based on an original story by Angela Russell
Art direction and mandalas by Angela Russell
Book design and illustrations by Bryn Barnard
www.brynbarnard.com
Andrea von Botefuhr photograph by Dr. Carl Botefuhr

Library of Congress Cataloging-in-Publication Data
von Botefuhr, Andrea.
The Land of Smaerd
by Andrea von Botefuhr. Illustrated by Bryn Barnard

Summary: The story of a extraordinary world
where dreams become realized, and all things are possible.

ISBN 978-0-615-18112-7 (trade)
[1.Dreams-Fiction] 1. Title

KNOW WONDER
PUBLISHING™

MANUFACTURED IN CHINA
First Edition
September 2008

THE LAND OF SMAERD

by Andrea von Botefuhr

illustrated by Bryn Barnard
with mandalas by Angela Russell

Know Wonder Publishing

In loving memory of "Grandpa Carl",
surely one of the greatest dreamers of them all!

We dedicate this book with deepest heartfelt gratitude
to Lucky and Anita, for believing in us …

and to Jack, for breathing life into our dream.

THE LAND OF SMAERD

nce upon a time

there was a land called Smaerd.

To an ordinary person Smaerd might seem quite weird.
You see, Smaerd is where dreams live
when they're not busy coming true …

this is where they wait, to be dreamed up by you.

While they are resting they take many shapes,
like butterflies or blue whales or big silly apes ...

or fairies, or gnomes, or big ice cream cones,
or long winding roads made of old cobblestones.

Sometimes they are clouds, all misty and white.
Sometimes they are rainbows, full of colorful light.

Dreams take all kinds of shapes when they have nothing else to do,
but of course they are happiest when they are busy coming true.

Dreams want to come true... it's the thing they do best.
Dreams love to be busy... they don't need much rest.

There are cute little houses for dreams that are small
and huge glorious castles for the biggest dreams of all.

In the gardens, fruits and vegetables
are abundant and blooming,
yet the seotatop and storrac
never need pruning.

I went to their school to see what I could learn,
but what was written on the board was hard to discern.

Then I figured it out and it filled me with laughter.
You see, their words are like ours…
but most are spelled backwards.

So I wrote the word Smaerd…then I turned it around.
Try it yourself, and see what I found.

In Smaerd... they don't have hospitals,
because no one gets bugs.
The doctors cure bad dreams with kisses and hugs.

People in Smaerd come in all shapes and sizes,
all colors of races and they're full of surprises

It's not just their job, it's their preoccupation
to grant dreams to dreamers in every kingdom and nation.

They register each dream keeping every detail in mind
and they stamp "First Priority" for dreamers who've been kind.

The rest of the dreams are kept track of by number...
the numbers are assigned to every oldster and youngster.

There are so many dreams in Smaerd, always coming and going...
they sprout from the seeds that dreamers are sowing.

And although a dream's life is extraordinarily fun,
there's an occasional mishap before a dream's day is done.

There once was a scream from a boy named Randall.
It seems he got a dream that he just couldn't handle.
You see, several sweet dreams had become so excited
on the way to their dreamers they accidentally collided.

They got all mixed up, all tangled and knotted
and in their confusion were neither fixed up nor spotted.
They were tumbled and thrown… they lost their direction.
They couldn't find their way home to make a correction.

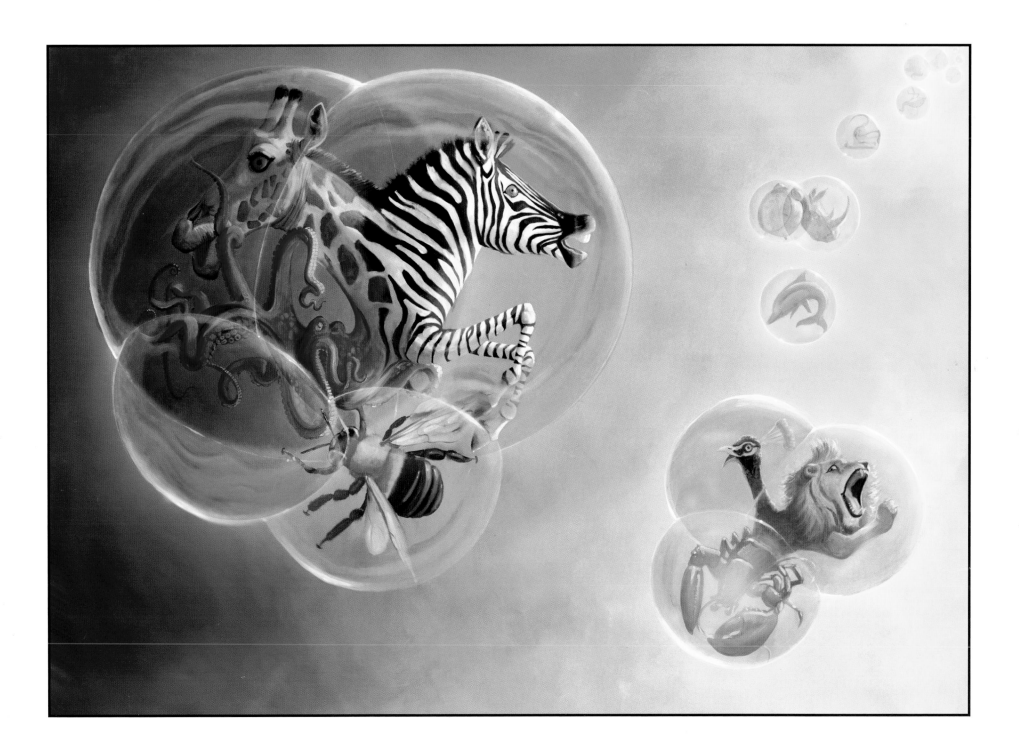

They arrived in odd forms, too frightening to mention
but to be a bad dream was not their intention.

Luckily, Randall's parents kissed and hugged him,
which released those poor dreams,
and they no longer bugged him.

Meanwhile back in Smaerd, after such a collision,
the dreams were untangled with the utmost precision.

The dreams were quite shook up, as you can imagine...
so they hugged them and soothed them with tea made of jasmine.

So, the next time you awaken from a terrible dream,
don't shudder or cry... and try not to scream.

Just remember, this is not what the dream meant to do,
and the dream could quite possibly be more frightened than you!

If ever you dream something that seems too crazy or weird,
just take a deep breath, and send the dream back to Smaerd.

You can be sure that the "Smaerd dream dispatchers"
want your sweetest dreams to come true and live happily ever after.

Now get out your crayons... your paint, glitter and glue, and create pictures of dreams that you'd like to come true.

Remember, no dreams are impossible,
too big or too small.
Any dream can come true ...

any dream at all!